Poppy
the Pirate Dog's
New Shipmate

Poppy
the Pirate Dog's
New Shipmate

Liz Kessler

Illustrated by
Mike Phillips

Orion
Children's Books

First published in Great Britain in 2013
by Orion Children's Books
a division of the Orion Publishing Group Ltd
Orion House
5 Upper St Martin's Lane
London WC2H 9EA
An Hachette UK Company

1 3 5 7 9 10 8 6 4 2

The Orion Publishing Group's policy is to use papers that
are natural, renewable and recyclable products and made
from wood grown in sustainable forests. The logging and
manufacturing processes are expected to conform to the
environmental regulations of the country of origin.

A catalogue record for this book
is available from the British Library

Printed in China

www.orionbooks.co.uk

*Dedicated to the actual,
original George*

Contents

Chapter One

Poppy the Pirate Dog was bored.
She was home alone. Again.

The summer holidays
had been the best time
of her life. She'd worn
her pirate skull and
crossbones scarf with
pride.

She'd read books
about pirates with
Tim. She'd made
stashes of pirate
treasure with Suzy.

She'd even had her own pirate ship.

But now it was all over.

Tim and Suzy had gone back to school. Mum and Dad were at work.

Poppy's skull and crossbones scarf had been forgotten.

Poppy lay by the window. She saw
Suzy walking up the drive.

'Sorry, Poppy, I haven't got time
to play,' Suzy called.

Tim was halfway out of the door with a football under his arm. 'Sorry, Poppy, I haven't got time—'

Then he stopped. 'Are you okay?' he asked. 'Would you like to look for some pirate treasure?'

Poppy wagged her tail. At last, someone was going to play with her!

Tim and Poppy sat on the rug with their findings.

A lamb bone, left over from last night's dinner.

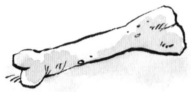

A squeaky plastic ball with lots of teeth marks.

And an old sock with a hole in the toe.

Poppy had an idea. She picked up the sock and took it to the sofa, pushing it under a cushion with her nose.

'Oh, I get it!' Tim said. 'You want us to hide the treasure!'

Poppy wagged her tail.

They took the squeaky ball into
Tim's bedroom and hid it in his
cupboard.

Then they took the lamb bone into
the garden and hid it behind the shed.

Tim stroked Poppy's head. 'That was fun, wasn't it?' He picked up his football and headed for the door.

Poppy was alone.

Again.

She tucked her tail between her legs and sloped back to bed.

Chapter Two

'I think Poppy's lonely,' said Tim,
over dinner.

Of course I'm lonely, Poppy thought. You try spending all day sitting alone in an empty house, and see how you feel.

'I think you're right,' said Suzy, as she tied the freshly-washed pirate scarf round Poppy's neck. 'Pirate dogs need a life of thrill and adventure, not an empty house.'

Exactly, Poppy thought. And they need someone to stay at home living the pirate life with them.

A shipmate who doesn't have to go to school or work.

Mum switched on the television.
Animal Rescue was about to start.

'Hold on,' Dad said. 'I think I might
have an idea.'

Next day was Saturday and Poppy was home by herself again. But she didn't mind this time. Something exciting was happening.

It had started with a phone call. Dad came off the phone and gathered everyone together. 'We can go straight over,' he said.

Tim knelt to stroke Poppy. 'We've got a surprise for you,' he said.

'You're going to have a little brother!' Suzy said.

A brother? Were they getting another Tim?

'We won't be long,' Mum called, as they all went out.

Poppy paced the house, wondering
what her new brother would be like.
Then she had a thought.

Tim was Suzy's brother.
If they were getting a little brother
for Poppy, that meant he'd be a
Dalmatian like her.

He would be her
shipmate, as well
as her brother.

She would teach
him all about being
a pirate dog.

She'd show him where to hide his treasure. She'd share her bed with him.

Maybe her family would get him a skull and crossbones scarf, just like hers.

Best of all, she wouldn't be alone any more.

'Poppy!' Dad called. 'We're home!
Come and meet your brother!'
   Poppy charged down the stairs.

'Poppy, this is George,' Suzy said.
She opened her arms wide enough
for Poppy to see. Poppy leapt up in
excitement.

Then she froze.
This couldn't be right.

Where were his spots? All Dalmatians had spots! He wasn't even black and white. He was … ginger!

Then Poppy noticed something else. This George wasn't even a dog.

He was … he was …

Suzy smiled. 'He's a kitten!'

Poppy knew about kittens from *Animal Rescue*. Kittens couldn't be pirates! They weren't nearly fierce or brave enough. What were her family thinking?

Poppy stared at the ball of ginger fluff in Suzy's arms. It had huge eyes, and little whiskers all round its mouth.

And at the end of its tiny paws,
reaching towards Poppy's nose,
it had –

Ouch! –

Claws!

And they hurt!

Suzy put George on the ground.

Poppy and George stared at each other. Then Poppy edged closer and leaned down to sniff him.

George reached a paw up and smacked Poppy right in the eye.

Huh! So much for her new shipmate! Poppy stomped over to her bed – and **didn't** make any space for George.

Chapter Three

When Poppy woke next morning, there was no one in sight. Usually, Tim or Suzy came for cuddles first thing.

Not this morning.

Everyone was in Mum and Dad's room, sitting on the bed.

They were all saying things like, 'Awww, he's so cute,' and, 'Oooh, look at his little paws.'

In the middle of the bed – right
where Poppy was never allowed to sit
– was a ball of ginger fluff. George!

Poppy put her head on the bed.

'Oh, Poppy, I didn't see you there,'
Tim said.

'Forgot all about you. We were
busy playing with your new brother,'
Dad said, laughing. The others
laughed with him.

Poppy didn't get the joke.

He's **not** my brother, she thought crossly. And he's definitely not my shipmate.

Chapter Four

'Are you sure Poppy and George will be OK together?' Tim asked as they left for school.

'They'll be fine,' Mum replied. 'Come on. We're going to be late.'

Poppy lay on her bed, more miserable than ever.

She could hear slurping sounds coming from the kitchen. She went to investigate.

George was having a drink – out of Poppy's water bowl!

Poppy growled and George looked up. He wiped his whiskers with one of his tiny fluffy paws and skipped away.

Poppy followed him into the lounge.
He had curled up on the sofa. Poppy
refused to look at him and headed to
her bed in the corner.

She closed her eyes and tried to
sleep. But she was too cross.

Then she heard a shuffling sound.

Poppy looked at the sofa. George was gone, but the pirate treasure she'd hidden with Tim, her sock, was on the sofa – and it was moving!

Poppy picked up the sock in
her teeth. It was heavier than she
remembered.

'Mmmiiiiiiaaaaaowwwwl!'

Poppy dropped the sock.
Something was inside it!
　　Something small and fluffy.
　　And ginger.

Poppy picked up the sock again and shook it. The tip of a ginger tail poked out. A ginger bottom and two ginger paws came next. One more shake and George plopped onto the floor.

Poppy let out a fierce growl. Well, as fierce as she could manage with a sock between her teeth.

She marched across the room,
dropped the sock on her bed and sat
on it. From now on, she would guard it
with her life!

At least George would never find
her other pirate treasures. They were
too well hidden.

Something was squeaking.

It was coming from Tim's bedroom.

Poppy went to see what it was.

Tim's wardrobe door was open. Inside, on top of Tim's PE kit, was George.

He was jumping up and down on the squeaky ball. Poppy's second piece of pirate treasure!

Poppy barked loudly. George froze. Paws in the air, ears sticking up, he looked at Poppy with his big, round eyes.

Poppy growled. She nosed George
out of the way and took her ball to her
bed. She would watch her treasure like
a hawk from now on.

She was just going to rest her eyes for a moment first. Protecting pirate treasure is hard work for anyone.

Chapter Five

Aaarrrrgggghhhh!
Something was pulling Poppy's tail.

George!

That was it! Poppy had had enough.
But before she could think anything
else, George leapt forwards and
pounced on her tail.

Poppy growled her most fearsome, angry, pirate growl.

George arched his back and let out a hiss that sounded like a snake.

Poppy stared at him for a moment in surprise.

Then she remembered how cross she was.

Barking, she chased George out of the room, across the hall and into the kitchen.

George jumped up and landed on the door handle.

The back door swung open.

Poppy barked again.

George slipped off the handle, fell to the ground and ran out into the garden.

Finally, thought Poppy. I've got the house to myself again.

Chapter Six

It was quiet. Too quiet.

Where was George? Making trouble
somewhere, probably.

Poppy went outside and sniffed the bushes. Not there. She tried the flowerbeds. Nothing there either.

Then she heard a noise around the back of the shed.

Nooooooo!

Poppy darted to her hiding place, and there was George, sitting on the wall – nibbling on her lamb bone!

Poppy jumped at the kitten, but
George bounded off the wall and away
through the flowers.

Poppy chased him round the
garden. She was going to teach that
kitten a lesson once and for all.

Before Poppy could catch him,
George dashed across the grass, leapt
high into the air – and landed on a lily
pad in the middle of the pond.

Poppy reached the edge of the
pond and skidded to a stop.

George was scrabbling around
on the lily pad. He was slipping, and
would soon end up in the water.

Good, thought Poppy. That'll
teach him to mess with Poppy the
Pirate Dog.

But even though she was a tough pirate dog, she couldn't help feeling sorry for him.

She couldn't leave him. She was supposed to look after him.

After all, he was her brother.

'Meowwwwl!' mewed George as a corner of the lily pad slipped under the water.

Poppy looked at the wooden
decking that led almost to the centre
of the pond.

There's nothing else for it, she
thought. I'll have to walk the plank.

Poppy tiptoed carefully all the way
to the end of the deck and stretched as
far as she could. George was just out
of reach.

George leaned towards Poppy.
The lily pad he was standing on sank
even more and George nearly sank
with it.

No! thought Poppy.

She thought she wouldn't make it, but then Poppy reached a bit further, grabbed George's neck in her teeth and pulled him to safety.

Chapter Seven

Poppy carried George along the plank and into the garden. She put him down on the grass.

Come on, little brother, she
thought. Let's get you inside.

Poppy picked up her lamb bone
and they went into the house.

Poppy took the bone to her bed.
She curled up next to it.

George sat on the floor.

'**Miaow**,' he said.

Poppy looked at him, then she
sighed and moved her treasure to
make a bit of space.

Come on then, she thought. Hop
aboard.

Suzy and Tim burst through the
door when they got in from school.

'George!' Suzy called.
'Poppy!' Tim shouted.

They ran into the lounge. Two warm bodies were snuggled cosily together, surrounded by a collection of pirate treasure.

'Mum, look!' Suzy called.

Mum came in the room. 'See,' she said. 'I told you Poppy would be fine with the kitten.'

He's not a kitten, Poppy thought,
pulling George a bit closer and snuggling
up a little tighter.

He's my new shipmate.